the things we keep from the light.

A Journey of Self-Discovery and Empowerment.

Raw 'n Rosy

ISBN: 978-1-961902-03-9

Printed in the United States of America

Cover design by Temika Mccanns

Editor and Illustrator: Elsie Bloomfield

Contents

Prelude

"Secrets in the dark,

hidden truths we keep,

a journey to the depths,

where souls begin to weep.

Pain and heartbreak,

struggles of self-discovery,

raw and honest words,

a story of true recovery.

Each turn of the page,

a new emotion to unfold,

inspiration and beauty,

in the stories yet untold.

Join us on this journey,

discover the power within,

as we navigate the things

we hide from the light within."

Chapter 1: Secrets

We hide our mistakes

Underneath the surface

Afraid to take the blame

Afraid of the consequences

We hide our past

In the corners of our minds

Afraid to confront it

Afraid to leave it behind

We hide our passions

In the corners of our minds

Afraid to chase them

Afraid of the unknown

We hide our longings

Deep within our hearts

Afraid to show the world

The depth of our wants

We hide our true selves

Behind a mask of who we think we should be

Afraid to show the world

Our authentic identity

We hide our mistakes,

Buried deep in the past

Afraid to take responsibility

Afraid of the judgement that will last

We hide our insecurities,

Deep within our hearts

Afraid to let them show

Afraid to be seen as weak, apart

We hide our true feelings,

Beneath a mask of indifference

Afraid to let them out

Afraid of the vulnerability and the sense

We hide our true desires,

Deep within our minds

Afraid to chase them,

Afraid of what we may find

We hide our true selves,

From the world and the light

But in doing so,

We deprive ourselves of the right

To be truly seen,

To be truly heard,

To live authentically,

To be who we truly are,

And to reach our full potentiality.

We hide our struggles,

Behind a facade of perfection

Afraid to show the world

Our true selves, in the reflection

We hide our secrets,

Deep within our souls

Afraid to let them out

Afraid of the unknown, the roles

We hide our past,

In the corners of our minds

Afraid to confront it

Afraid to leave it behind

But the truth is,

We can't hide forever,

We must face our fears,

And let our true selves be discovered

For it is only in embracing

Our true selves and our truths

That we can truly live,

And find the peace that eludes.

We hide our secrets

Deep in the shadows

Afraid to let them out

Afraid of what may follow

We hide our insecurities

Deep within our souls

Afraid to show vulnerability

Afraid of being exposed

We hide our true feelings

Behind a facade of stoicism

Afraid to show emotion

Afraid of being seen as weak

We hide our true desires

Deep in the depths of our hearts

Afraid to chase them

Afraid of what they may start

We hide our true selves

From the light

But in doing so

We deprive ourselves of the right

To be seen and heard

To live authentically

To be who we truly are

And to reach our full potentiality

Chapter 2: Emotions

We hide our insecurities

Deep within our hearts

Afraid to show the world

The parts of us that fall short

We hide our struggles

Behind a facade of perfection

Afraid to show the world

The work and effort we put in

We hide our sorrows

Deep beneath the surface

Afraid to confront them

Afraid of the hurt

We hide our fears

In the depths of our souls

Afraid to confront them

Afraid of being out of control

We hide our pain,

Deep within our hearts

Afraid to confront it

Afraid of falling apart

We hide our fear,

Beneath a mask of confidence

Afraid to show vulnerability

Afraid of the unknown sense

We hide our anger,

Deep in the depths of our soul

Afraid to let it out

Afraid of the damage it may dole

We hide our sadness,

Behind a facade of happiness

Afraid to show the world

Our true emotional state and its express

We hide our love,

Deep within our hearts

Afraid to let it out

Afraid of rejection and the depart

But the truth is,

Emotions are a part of life

And they shape who we are

We must face them head on,

And reach for a brighter star

We must learn to embrace

All of our emotions,

The good and the bad,

For it is only in doing so,

That we can truly live,

And find the peace that eludes.

We hide our regrets,

Deep beneath the surface

Afraid to confront them

Afraid of the hurt

We hide our guilt,

In the shadows of our mind

Afraid to take responsibility

Afraid of what we'll find

We hide our pain,

Deep within our hearts

Afraid to confront it

Afraid of falling apart

We hide our fear,

Beneath a mask of bravery

Afraid to show vulnerability

Afraid of what others may see

We hide our anger,

Deep in the depths of our soul

Afraid to let it out

Afraid of the harm it may dole

We hide our sadness,

Behind a facade of cheer

Afraid to show the world

Our true emotional state that is dear

We hide our love,

Deep within our hearts

Afraid to let it out

Afraid of rejection and the depart

But the truth is,

Emotions are a part of life

And they shape who we are

We must face them head on,

And reach for a brighter star

We must learn to accept

All of our emotions,

The good and the bad,

For it is only in doing so,

That we can truly live,

And find the peace that eludes.

We hide our regrets,

Deep beneath the surface

Afraid to confront them

Afraid of the hurt

We hide our guilt,

In the shadows of our mind

Afraid to take responsibility

Afraid of what we'll find

We must learn to forgive ourselves

And move forward

For it is only in doing so,

That we can truly live,

And find the peace that eludes.

We hide our love,

Deep within our hearts

Afraid to let it out

Afraid of rejection and the depart

We hide our joy,

Deep within our souls

Afraid to show it

Afraid of how it could be perceived

We must learn to let go

Of the fear and doubts

And embrace all of our emotions

For it is only in doing so

That we can truly live

And find the peace that eludes.

We hide our vulnerability,

Deep within our hearts

Afraid to show the world

The parts of us that fall apart

We hide our insecurities,

In the corners of our mind

Afraid to confront them

Afraid of being left behind

We hide our true feelings,

Deep within our souls

Afraid to show the world

Our true selves, whole

But the truth is,

Our emotions make us human

And they shape our experiences

We must learn to embrace them

And let them be our guides

We must learn to accept

All of our emotions,

The good and the bad

For it is only in doing so

That we can truly live

And find the peace that eludes.

We must learn to let go

Of the fear and doubts

And embrace all of our emotions

For it is only in doing so

That we can truly live

And find the peace that eludes.

We must learn to be honest

With ourselves and others

And let go of the need

To hide from our emotions,

For it is only in doing so

That we can truly live

And find the peace that eludes.

We must learn to accept

Our past mistakes

And move forward

For it is only in doing so,

That we can truly live,

And find the peace that eludes.

Chapter 3: Pain

We hide our doubts

Deep within our minds

Afraid to take a chance

Afraid of what we'll find

We hide our secrets

Deep within our hearts

Afraid to let them out

Afraid of the dark

We hide our pain

Behind a mask of smiles

Afraid to show the world

Our true selves for a while

We hide our scars

Deep beneath the surface

Afraid to show the world

The pain that made them

We hide our hurt,

Deep within our hearts

Afraid to confront it

Afraid of falling apart

We hide our wounds,

Beneath a mask of strength

Afraid to show weakness

Afraid of the length

We hide our scars,

Deep in the depths of our soul

Afraid to let them be seen

Afraid of the toll

We hide our suffering,

Behind a facade of smiles

Afraid to show the world

Our true emotional trials

We hide our pain,

Deep within our hearts

Afraid to confront it

Afraid of falling apart

But the truth is,

Pain is a part of life

And it shapes who we are

We must face it head on

And reach for a brighter star

We must learn to embrace

All of our pain

For it is in facing it

That we can truly gain

The strength and growth

That comes from overcoming

And find the peace

That eludes.

We hide our grief,

Deep beneath the surface

Afraid to confront it

Afraid of the hurt

We hide our trauma,

In the shadows of our mind

Afraid to confront it

Afraid of being confined

We must learn to heal

From our past hurt

And move forward

For it is only in doing so

That we can truly live

And find the peace that eludes.

We hide our hurt,

Deep within our hearts

Afraid to confront it

Afraid of falling apart

We hide our wounds,

Beneath a mask of invincibility

Afraid to show weakness

Afraid of being seen as vulnerable

We hide our scars,

Deep in the depths of our soul

Afraid to let them be seen

Afraid of the toll

We hide our suffering,

Behind a facade of contentment

Afraid to show the world

Our true emotional discontentment

We hide our pain,

Deep within our hearts

Afraid to confront it

Afraid of falling apart

But the truth is,

Pain is a part of life

And it shapes who we are

We must face it head on

And reach for a brighter star

We must learn to embrace

All of our pain

For it is in facing it

That we can truly gain

The strength and growth

That comes from overcoming

And find the peace

That eludes.

We hide our grief,

Deep beneath the surface

Afraid to confront it

Afraid of the hurt

We hide our trauma,

In the shadows of our mind

Afraid to confront it

Afraid of being confined

We must learn to heal

From our past hurt

And move forward

For it is only in doing so

That we can truly live

And find the peace that eludes.

We must learn to let go

Of the past pain

And allow ourselves

To feel and grow again

For it is only in doing so

That we can truly live

And find the peace that eludes.

We must learn to be kind

To ourselves and our healing

And understand that pain

Is a necessary part of the feeling.

We hide our brokenness,

Deep within our hearts

Afraid to confront it

Afraid of falling apart

We hide our wounds,

Beneath a facade of invincibility

Afraid to show vulnerability

Afraid of being seen as weak

We hide our scars,

Deep in the depths of our soul

Afraid to reveal them

Afraid of the toll they may take on our whole

We hide our anguish,

Behind a mask of happiness

Afraid to show the world

Our true emotional distress

We hide our pain,

Deep within our hearts

Afraid to confront it

Afraid of the suffering it imparts

But the truth is,

Pain is a natural part of life

And it shapes and molds us

We must face it head on

And find the light in the fuss

We must learn to embrace

All of our pain

For it is through facing it

That we can truly gain

The understanding, wisdom and strength

That comes from overcoming

And find the peace

That eludes.

We hide our grief,

Deep beneath the surface

Afraid to confront it

Afraid of the hurt it may disperse

We hide our trauma,

In the shadows of our mind

Afraid to confront it

Afraid of being trapped and confined

We must learn to heal

From our past hurt

And move forward

For it is only in doing so

That we can truly live

And find the peace that eludes.

Chapter 4: Desires

We hide our passions,

Deep within our hearts

Afraid to chase them

Afraid of where they may start

----

we hide our fire

behind a mask of fear

afraid to let it out

afraid of what it may bring here

we hide our voice

behind a wall of silence

afraid to speak up

afraid of the violence

we hide our truth

behind a web of lies

afraid to be vulnerable

afraid of the ties

we hide our dreams

behind a cloak of doubt

afraid to chase them

afraid of what it's all about

but the truth is

our desires are meant to be followed

for they are the compass

to our lives that are hallowed

we must learn to trust

our own hearts and desires

for it is only in doing so

that we can truly find

our own fire and set the world on fire.

we hide our passion

behind a mask of apathy

afraid to let it out

afraid of the intensity

we hide our hope

behind a facade of cynicism

afraid to believe

afraid of the vulnerability within

we hide our purpose

behind a wall of confusion

afraid to take action

afraid of the illusion

we hide our aspirations

behind a cloak of complacency

afraid to strive for more

afraid of the energy

but the truth is

our desires are meant to be pursued

for they are the driving force

of the life we are meant to choose

we must learn to listen

to the whispers of our hearts

and chase our dreams

for it is only in doing so

that we can truly find

our own purpose and make a start.

We hide our dreams,

Beneath a mask of practicality

Afraid to pursue them

Afraid of their unpredictability

We hide our aspirations,

Deep in the depths of our soul

Afraid to let them out

Afraid of the unknown and the toll

We hide our desires,

Behind a facade of contentment

Afraid to show the world

Our true yearning and the extent

We hide our ambitions,

Deep within our hearts

Afraid to chase them

Afraid of where they may start

But the truth is,

Our desires make us who we are

And they shape our aspirations

We must learn to embrace them

And let them guide us to new horizons

We must learn to accept

All of our desires

The big and the small

For it is only in doing so

That we can truly live

And find the fulfillment that calls.

We hide our aspirations,

Deep beneath the surface

Afraid to confront them

Afraid of the hurt

We hide our goals,

In the shadows of our mind

Afraid to chase them

Afraid of being left behind

We must learn to pursue

Our dreams and goals

And move forward

For it is only in doing so

That we can truly live

And find the peace that eludes.

We hide our passions,

In the corners of our mind,

Afraid to chase them,

Afraid to be confined.

We hide our secrets,

Deep within our hearts,

Afraid to let them out,

Afraid of the dark.

We hide our longings,

Deep within our hearts,

Afraid to show the world,

The depth of our wants.

We hide our sorrows,

Deep beneath the surface,

Afraid to confront them,

Afraid of the hurt.

We hide our fears,

In the depths of our souls,

Afraid to confront them,

Afraid of being out of control.

We hide our doubts,

Deep within our minds,

Afraid to take a chance,

Afraid of what we'll find.

We hide our pain,

Behind a mask of smiles,

Afraid to show the world,

Our true selves for a while.

We hide our creativity,

Deep within our hearts

Afraid to express it

Afraid of where it may start

We hide our hopes,

Beneath a mask of realism

Afraid to dream big

Afraid of the unknown and the schism

We hide our purpose,

Deep in the depths of our soul

Afraid to let it out

Afraid of the unknown and the toll

We hide our aspirations,

Behind a facade of contentment

Afraid to show the world

Our true yearning and the extent

We hide our ambitions,

Deep within our hearts

Afraid to chase them

Afraid of where they may start

But the truth is,

Our desires and aspirations are a part of us

And they shape our lives and our future

We must learn to embrace them

And let them guide us to new adventures

We must learn to accept

All of our desires

The big and the small

For it is only in doing so

That we can truly live

And find the fulfillment that calls.

We hide our talents,

Deep beneath the surface

Afraid to showcase them

Afraid of the judgement and the curse

We hide our passions,

In the shadows of our mind

Afraid to pursue them

Afraid of being left behind

We must learn to trust

Our own abilities and passions

And move forward

For it is only in doing so

That we can truly live

And find the peace that eludes.

We've all got secrets

we keep in the dark

things we hide from the light

that leave us with scars

But in the shadows

we find the courage

to speak our truth

and let our voice be heard

In the darkness

we find the strength

to rise above

and become who we're meant to be

We've all got secrets

but it's in the sharing

that we find the power

to heal and be free

So let go of the past

and embrace the present

for it's in the letting go

that we find true empowerment

And it's in the sharing

of the things we hide from the light

that we find the courage

to live a life truly bright.

About the book

"Things We keep From the Light" is a powerful and emotional poetry collection that delves into the hidden truths that we keep buried deep inside. It explores the themes of healing, self-love, forgiveness, and empowerment. Through the use of raw and honest language, the author takes us on a journey of self-discovery as they share their own experiences of overcoming pain and rising above. The book is divided into four chapters, each one delving deeper into the emotions that we hide from the light. It is an honest and relatable work that will resonate with readers of all ages. This poetry collection is not just a book, it's a journey to self-discovery, healing, and empowerment. It's a reminder that the beauty in the world lies in the rising after the fall. It's time to let go of the past, embrace the present and be who we're meant to be.